MURDER BY MOONLIGHT

A COLLECTION OF SHORT STORIES

DIANA RUBINO

Copyright (C) 2021 Diana Rubino

Layout design and Copyright (C) 2021 by Next Chapter

Published 2021 by Magnum Opus – A Next Chapter Imprint

Edited by Brice Fallon

Cover art by CoverMint

This book is a work of fiction. Names, characters, places, and incidents are the product of the author's imagination or are used fictitiously. Any resemblance to actual events, locales, or persons, living or dead, is purely coincidental.

All rights reserved. No part of this book may be reproduced or transmitted in any form or by any means, electronic or mechanical, including photocopying, recording, or by any information storage and retrieval system, without the author's permission.

SOUVENIR

A MORTAR SHELL hit the ground and exploded. A blinding flash lit up the night sky, illuminating five startled faces inside the old farmhouse.

The second shell scored a direct hit, rocking the house to its foundations. As debris scattered everywhere, the explosive force splintered the wooden table. Maps, documents, books, and computers flew across the room.

The men scrambled for their weapons—all except Hani Terif. He frantically searched the rubble for a vital item. "Let me find it, please!" he begged.

As he scrabbled in the shards of wood, paper, melted plastic, and metal, his trained ear distinguished each sound; even above their own spitting and coughing weapons. Mortars plopped in the distance. Shells screeched over the rasp of American-made automatic rifles. As fifty-caliber machine guns gargled with rifle fire, he froze. This meant one thing: Israeli commandos, too many to fight off. They must escape now or face certain death.

With their aging Russian weapons and limited ammunition, he and his fellow Deadly Underground brethren had no chance against their attackers. The best-trained soldiers on this side of the world, the Israeli commandos closed in fast. Their life spans possibly reduced to a handful of seconds, his men fought their way out. They crawled, dragging wounded legs. They limped, arms slung around comrades' shoulders.

"Meet me at the Deadly Underground safe house outside Cairo in two weeks!" Hani ordered his men. "I will hold off the enemy for as long as possible."

Rockets roared overhead in a dreadful barrage. His muscles tightened. Knowing he would never hear the shot that killed him, he trembled. The others charged out into the night, under cover of his prattling machine gun fire. Israeli bullets whispered around their feet. He continued to scan the room for the priceless Koran. Finally, his sharp eyes spotted it wedged under a corner of the rug. Grateful for keen eyesight, he leapt across the room to grasp the small leather-bound book.

He fled the building as an explosion blew it sky-high. Watching his fellow brothers-in-arms blown to shards of bone and spattered blood, Hani realized he was the only survivor.

The British Airways 747 headed for London with its payload of American tourists, British visitors eager to return home, fidgety first-time flyers, and a genial crew. The Lassiter Tours group sat in coach; six Americans of various ages and backgrounds, about to embark on their whirlwind tour of Egypt.

Settled in a window seat, Dr. Lawrence Everett, Professor of Heritage Studies at Plymouth State University read a thesis on his iPad. Next to him sat his wife Janice, silently mouthing a Hail Mary, rosary beads clutched between her fingers.

Professor Everett noticed his wife's bowed head. "Honey,

we're not even off the ground yet." Just in case, he reached for the plastic-lined bag in the pouch in front of her.

"Hey, we're finally moving!" Jeff Sullivan, the passenger to Janice Everett's right, nudged her. "We're now on the way to our first fuel stop: London Heathrow," he dictated into a digital recorder. "From there we'll continue on to Cairo, Egypt. The origin of all genius known to mankind..."

Across the aisle, in the middle three seats, sat the Brooklyn-born Russo family: ample-paunched Dominic, his health-conscious wife Anna Maria, and their twenty-two-year-old daughter Carmella, reading *Yoga Journal*. This trip was a celebration of Carmella's second chance at life.

The jet climbed into the clouds, about to blaze its vapor trail across the Atlantic.

The Lassiter Tours group arrived at the Cairo Hilton in time for a late dinner. After the hurried meal in the hotel's restaurant, the tour director arrived.

"Good evening. I'm Yasar Massri. I'm an Egyptian archaeology student and will be your guide for the next two weeks."

The travelers gathered in the hotel lobby as Yasar gave a brief history of Memphis, their first stop the following morning. "Please be here in the lobby at eight-thirty to meet our motor coach," he finished his spiel of instructions. "Breakfast will be served at eight."

As the crowd shuffled toward the elevators, Carmella approached Yasar, now entering the lounge. "You sound like a learned man of the world." She rushed out her words, breathless with excitement. "I can't wait to see Egypt."

"I take it you've never been here before." He moved towards her, closing the respectable distance.

"No, never. This is a very special trip for me. A real celebration. I've always been fascinated with Egyptian history and the mystery of the pyramids, how they're built with such precision, lined up with stars. You sure have a history to be proud of."

He beamed. "Well, thank you. We are proud of it."

"Whenever I travel, I make sure to meet the locals. Especially the tour guides." She paused for effect—and to take a breath. "Would you like to sit in the lounge and talk a while? I'll even take notes." She slid her iPad from her bag to show him.

"I'd be happy to." He led her into the lounge where they took two seats at a cozy corner table. He ordered a beer and she ordered orange juice.

"Speaking of history, look at this." He slid a small leather book from his pocket and held it out to her.

She stared in wonder as he placed it in her palm. "It's so old and fragile. Was it found in a pharaoh's tomb or something?"

He chuckled. "No, it's a Koran. I bought it at an auction this morning. It somehow survived a battle between Israeli commandos and terrorists at the old Bishara farm, a few months back."

She opened it and ran a finger down the inside cover. "It's so frayed and—what's this writing here?"

"I'm not sure. I need to study it closer." The waiter served their drinks. Yasar took a sip of his beer.

"Did you pay a lot for it, if you don't mind my asking?" She opened it to a random page and swept her eyes over the ancient, foreign writing.

"About one hundred dollars, American money. The other bidders had been village sightseers, too scared of the terrorists of Deadly Underground to even bid for the few intact items. As if they'd kill for the wreckage of their junk." He chuckled.

"Well, it certainly is something to be treasured." She held the precious artifact between two fingers and placed it in his hands.

"I know it will protect me from any harm. It sounds superstitious, but that's the feeling I have about it, from the moment I saw it." He clasped it and held it to his heart.

Carmella smiled. "Oh, I know all about that. No one's more superstitious than Old World Italians. I've seen old folks cast the *Malocchio*, the evil eye, when they have it in for someone." She pointed her index finger and pinkie at him.

"I hope that doesn't mean you just gave it to me." He shielded his face with his Koran, laughing.

"Not at all." She circled her hand around her glass. "I never wish harm on anyone. It's bad karma. You know all about that, don't you?"

He nodded. "Oh, do I. I respect God, worship Him, and fear Him. And His wrath. If you call it karma, so be it."

That sent a shiver down her spine. "Let's talk about something pleasant, like your history. I can't wait to see the pyramids and all the ancient artifacts."

They spent the evening chatting about history, art, books. She lost track of time.

What a nice guy, she thought, returning to her hotel room. *I hope he's on Facebook. He's worth getting to know better.*

The next morning, a motor coach waited outside the front entrance of the Cairo Hilton while Yasar rushed the American tourists through their breakfast. "We must now board the bus, folks. It's time to roll."

As they gulped down their coffee and hurried out the door, Dominic Russo wrapped the remaining croissants in a napkin and stuffed them into his pocket with packets of jelly. The bus started up and headed for Memphis, stopping briefly so Yasar and the driver could face Mecca and pray. Yasar would not be the only Muslim on board and all were expected to heed the call to prayer.

Throngs of tourists surrounded the enormous statue of Ramses II, lying on its back inside a gazebo-like structure. Yasar's cell phone rang and he glanced at the screen. "Please stick together, folks, I will return in a moment," he instructed the group. He dashed away to take the call. The tourists continued ogling the statue and cartouche, the rectangular-shaped design with Ramses's name in hieroglyphics. After ten minutes, only Carmella noticed Yasar hadn't returned.

"Where's Yasar?" A stab of fear shot through her. She knew how dangerous the Middle East was. They'd taken this trip against the State Department's warning to stay away. Her eyes darted about as she dashed outside and lowered her sunglasses, scanning the area for the handsome tour guide.

Moments later, a policeman appeared, holding something in his hand. His narrowed eyes scanned the crowd. To her mounting horror, Carmella saw he held a bright yellow tour group badge. Her heart leapt to her throat as the officer spotted the matching badge pinned to Carmella's chest. She swayed, nearly fainting as he approached her group.

"Ladies and gentlemen," he stammered in faltering English. "Your tour guide, Yasar...he is dead."

Carmella broke down and wept. Dominic Russo's jaw clamped shut on the croissant he'd been munching. Janice Everett gasped and knelt on the ground to pray.

Dominic stepped up to the policeman. "How did he die?"

Jeff Sullivan dug through his bag for his digital recorder.

"It was apparently a poisoning."

"It's this water…the water here, they told us not to drink it!" Anna Maria Russo stuffed two Vitamin C tablets into her mouth.

"Ma'am, the water here is poison only to foreigners," the officer explained. "Yasar was Egyptian."

"Then it was the curse of the Pharaoh!" Janice Everett shrieked, clasping her worry-worn rosary beads.

Numb with shock, Carmella followed the group back to the bus, and sat in stunned silence all the way back to Cairo.

She'd only spent a few hours of her life with Yasar, but thoroughly enjoyed his company. What made her shudder was a sudden thought: he'd been so sure that small Koran would protect him from harm.

Was that tattered book cursed in some way? She shook the horrible thought from her mind. Now *that's* Old-World superstition.

A detective arrived at the hotel after dinner to interview the tour group and take statements. After he thanked them and left, she didn't contribute to her group's indignant griping: "What does he think we are, murderers?" "How dare he talk to Americans like this!" "I wish I had my lawyer here!"

A replacement tour guide arrived at the hotel the next morning; another Egyptian student named Samir. "Yasar and I had been good friends," he told the group, his dark eyes brimming with tears. "I am deeply grieved over his untimely death."

The magnificent pyramids loomed ahead, towering into the cloudless blue sky. The ancient Sphinx crouched in the sand. Samir led the travelers on foot to the pyramid of King Khufu as camels trotted alongside them, their riders barking offers to snap their photos for a mere $20.

"If anyone is claustrophobic, stay outside rather than brave the dark, narrow passageway inside the pyramid," Samir warned. Carmella opted to stay outside. The other travelers entered the tomb, crouched forward, and disappeared inside. Samir turned towards Mecca and prayed.

Twenty minutes later, the tourists emerged. But Samir was nowhere to be seen.

"Where's Samir?" Professor Everett polished his glasses with a shoeshine cloth from the hotel.

Carmella's heart slammed. She searched her companions' haunted faces. *Oh, no.* An ominous disquiet hovered over the group like a thundercloud.

An ambulance screeched to a halt beside the tour bus. Two stretcher bearers rounded the Pyramid and returned carrying a body wrapped in a blood-spattered sheet. Just like last time, a trailing policeman held a familiar yellow badge in his hand, this one spattered with gore.

Carmella's knees buckled. She sobbed, not just out of grief for the two senseless killings, but fear stabbed her like a dagger.

She couldn't help but wonder: *Who's next?*

"We've got to find a priest," Janice Everett wailed while Jeff Sullivan reported the news into his recorder.

Once again, a detective interviewed the group and took notes. This time they were too flabbergasted to complain or wish for lawyers. They sat, faces frozen, eyeing each other. It seemed no one wanted to rouse more suspicion by being the first to get up and leave.

So, Carmella got up to leave. After all, she knew she was innocent. "I hope they find out who committed these horrible crimes," she stated. "G'night, folks." She nodded at her parents, turned and strode into the bar for a good stiff one.

"I'm Antonio Calabrese, your new tour guide, and tomorrow our first stop will be the Cairo Museum." The wavy-haired Italian greeted the American travelers in the hotel lounge later that evening. He went on to review the history of Tutankhamen's tomb, discovered in 1922 by Howard Carter, and the many deaths attributed to the 'curse' of the Pharaoh. "But that's *pazzo*." Grinning, he circled a finger around the side of his head. "There's no such things as curses." The others nodded in full agreement, joining him in laughter and ridicule, blowing it off as wacko. To Carmella, their laughter sounded hollow and forced, as if they tried too hard to forget the horror of the preceding days.

Carmella didn't laugh. Not that she believed in curses—her mind dwelled on something else. Some otherworldly instinct told her she'd known Antonio before. Maybe not in this life, but she was so drawn to him, she sensed they shared a powerful cosmic connection. Were they related? Hey, with all the inbreeding in Southern Italy, a common surname was the last way people discovered their kinfolk.

She had no Calabreses in her family tree, but that meant nothing. In all likelihood, they shared the same bloodline. Her inner voice repeated *I know you* so many times, she began mouthing those words silently as he addressed the group.

He scanned each face, and for an instant his eyes met hers. He looked away, but she kept a steady gaze on him.

She crossed her legs, swinging her foot back and forth. A few minutes later he looked her way again, spotted her and winked. She smiled. He looked away. She watched his every move. He made elaborate Italian hand gestures as he described the history with zeal and passion. A rock song with a steady beat pulsed through the lounge speakers. She started to sway to the music. She tapped her foot. Their bodies moved in exact rhythm with each other. Their eyes met again.

This time they locked.

After dinner, her parents went to the lounge for cocktails, but Carmella stayed in the room to catch up with her social media sites. At about 9:00, she heard a knock at the door. Expecting her parents, she opened it, but took a step back in surprise. "Wow, now this is what I call room service!"

"Ciao, Carmella." Antonio Calabrese's hair matched his eyes, a deep chocolate bon bon brown, his complexion bronzed by a south-of-Italy sun. He wasn't much taller than she, but his build showed that he took care of what he had.

"I've been wanting to meet you and...well, I hope I'm not disturbing you." He looked over her shoulder into the room. "Your parents told me to come on up. I hope I'm not being too forward. They did warn me that you're a tough Brooklyn girl, not that I have any impure intentions..."

She thanked God she hadn't put her hair in those awful pink electric curlers she dragged everywhere. She held the door open for him. "You can never be too forward, Antonio. We have volumes to talk about." Somehow she knew this wouldn't send him running. This was not some chance encounter. This was the first night of the rest of their lives together. "Please come in."

"*Grazie.*" He settled in a chair in the sitting area.

She perched on the sofa, a respectable distance away. "The universe is shaping both our destinies at this very moment, you know," she informed him, a strange thing to say to someone she'd known for 20 minutes. But it was entirely appropriate—and true.

"I picked up on it, too, when you connected with me earlier in the lounge. Otherwise, I wouldn't be here." His soothing voice caressed her ears.

"I'm sorry I didn't introduce myself sooner, but I had to do some studying. I'm working on a Master's degree in the History of Art and Archaeology and I fit tours in between classes and exams." He sat back and crossed his ankle over his knee.

"Well, so am I. I'm studying for a Master's in Women's History at New York University. Although I'm an artist at heart. A writer, but I call it art."

"I'm an artist, too. I paint in oils." He glanced at her iPad. "If you can do that later, why don't we go down to the lounge for a drink?"

"How about going somewhere we won't have to sit with my parents?" She stood and grabbed her jacket. "Do you know any places we can duck into?"

She'd duck into one of the Pyramids with him if it were open. Anything for their souls to meld and connect. The way it was meant to be.

Seated at a wooden table for two in a dimly lit bar, orange juice before her, a glass of wine before him, Antonio very unshyly opened up the conversation.

"So, you're abstaining tonight? Or is it part of an early breakfast?"

"No." She sipped her juice. "I'm on the wagon permanently. I don't drink at all."

Antonio fingered the chain around his neck, a gold Christ

head suspended from it. "I drink wine and beer but don't do any drugs. I know everybody's got a..." He searched for a word.

"Vice."

He nodded. "Ah, *si*. Or maybe quirk?" He took a sip of wine. "Why don't you drink? Does it make you sick?"

"No, it goes deeper than that. My best friend was killed in a car accident. Hit by a drunk driver." She spoke freely, without breaking down in tears. It wasn't painful to talk about it with him. She found it cathartic to share one of her tragic losses with him. She'd share much more later. "But you go right ahead and drink. Just don't overdo it."

Their first meeting and she was already giving him orders! But it rolled off her tongue as naturally as saying his name. He laughed, showing his gleaming moonlight smile. "I obey, *Consigliere*."

"It's for your own good. I—" She'd been about to say "I care about you" but shut her mouth, cutting off that confession. She'd never experienced love at first sight, but now she knew—this was a powerful connection. She and Antonio Calabrese had shared a far distant journey.

Antonio stared into his wine glass, as if crystal-ball gazing. He raised his head and their eyes met. "Did you visit Salerno last April?"

"No, but I went to Rome and Milan the summer before. Why?"

"Nothing, I—" He swirled the wine in his glass, their eyes still locked. "I thought I saw you there then. I could've sworn I saw you. If it wasn't you, you have a twin."

"We're all supposed to have a double." But a double of him? Well, maybe south of Rome...

He winked at her. Her cheeks blazed. "I'll blurt it out, Antonio. We've never met, not in Italy, not in this life, but I know you. You'll see what I mean as the tour continues. I don't want to say any more now because it leaves too much room for doubt, but by the end of the tour, you'll realize what I'm saying is the honest truth."

"I already do know." He grasped her hand on the tabletop. "Let's talk about you. What did you do in Rome and Milan that summer?"

"I have relatives in Formello. I visit them every year if I can. We take side trips all over Italy and the continent. I'd hoped to find you on one of those trips."

"And we meet in Egypt. How strange is that?" He shook his head, a dreamy smile on his lips.

"It's not strange at all. Just the opposite," she countered, studying his dimples. "Because our paths were meant to cross." The dainty sip of juice she took became a gulp. She sputtered.

"Are you all right?" He leaned forward.

"Yeah, just..." She coughed and cleared her throat. "Went down the wrong way. This vacation has been one unreal thing after another. I mean., you and I meeting here, and me with this feeling of déjà vu."

"If you say so." He smiled and smoothed back his hair. "I can't say I feel I've met you before. I don't meet beautiful girls like you very often. In fact, hardly ever."

She muttered a "thank you" between more sips.

"I'd love to see some of your work," he said. "What kind of material do you write?"

"Biographies. I was going to write genre fiction, but I stuck with history. I'm researching Lucrezia Borgia."

"I'm not up on writer's—" He pressed his thumb and fingertips together and moved his hand back and forth in the classic Italian gesture. "How you say—jargon. What did you say it was?"

"Biography," she answered. "Factual stories, no fiction."

"No, that French word." He swatted the air.

She held up her index finger. "Oh, genre. That means category. Westerns, mysteries, romances; they're all genres."

He nodded. "It's like that with art, too. There's Cubism, Impressionism," he counted on his fingers, "Futurism, all the 'ism's', then there's the Bauhaus...dozens of them. Except they're called movements." He cocked a brow and tilted his head, squeezing her hand. "We must see each other's work."

A rush of emotions—amazement, affection, the stirrings of love—surged through her heart, warming her. "Oh, *si, si*," she whispered. "And I'm a huge art aficionado. What kind of paintings do you do?"

His eyes never left hers. "These days, portraits of wealthy Egyptians."

She halted her glass midway to her mouth. "Why?"

"Well, it is against all odds that I came to live here. I used to paint landscapes in oils when I lived at home. I tried entering my paintings in art shows, tried selling them in galleries, stores, anywhere. No one wanted them. I couldn't give them away. So, after several years of rejection after rejection, and cruel ridicule from everyone, including my own family, I gave up." He released a sigh. "I flung my paintings in the trash. A rich Egyptian woman on holiday walked past my house and spotted my paintings in the trash. She knocked on my door and told me how much she admired my work. She hired me to paint scenes of Egypt."

"How could you if you'd never been here before?"

He flashed a smile. "She brought me here. I now work for her, her family, and her friends, painting Egyptian sunrises and sunsets, boats on the Nile, the pyramids, the Sphinx, all the other great sites. I've earned enough to continue my education here. The tour guiding is an easy way to earn credits towards my Master's degree." He gave her a nod. "So that is why I am here, against all odds. Because a benevolent soul found my work in the trash and believed in me."

She let out a low whistle. "Wow, what a story. Now it's my turn. I'm here against all odds, too."

His brows shot up and his eyes lit up. "And of course, I need to know your story now that I've shared mine."

"My friend Pete had a private pilot's license. We went for a joyride in his Piper Saratoga. It crashed." Her voice faltered.

"Oh, *dio*," he whispered.

"Mechanical malfunction, something...he was killed. I survived. I had some serious injuries, but I survived. When I was recovering in the hospital, I had a dream about him. He always wanted to come here, always joked that his plane wouldn't make it to Egypt, but in the dream, he asked me to come here for him. So here I am. Celebrating my second chance at life. I don't call it a brush with death."

"You're here for a fated reason, then." His nod assured her.

"No, I'm here for two fated reasons. I was meant to meet you. And nothing is going to ruin that. But..." She winced as a stab of fear pierced her gut. *God, please don't let him meet a tragic end like the last two guides,* she silently prayed. She took a deep breath before blurting it out. "I hope you know what's happened to our last two tour guides. The rumors range from crimes of passion to the curse of the Pharaoh. We don't know what to think anymore." Her voice quivered. She clenched her fists to keep from trembling.

"I'm not worried." He smiled, white teeth gleaming against tanned skin. "I'm safe from any Egyptian curse. I'm Italian."

"That's rather cavalier." She trembled as fear refused to stop hovering over her. "I believe curses are silly, but I do believe bad energy is harmful—and deadly. What someone calls a curse may just be bad energy or an evil entity out to harm you. As long as there's good energy, there must also be bad." Her voice steadied as she talked and calmed a bit. "But you seem to be very...grounded." She looked into his eyes and saw the intelligence there. *No, this guy's not a believer in curses, or even karma*, she thought with a secret smile.

Those intelligent eyes lit up. "That is a perfect word, grounded. I was always told I'm earthy. Same difference I suppose." He looked at his watch and she crashed back down to Earth, the constraints of time shattering the magic of their encounter. "I need to study some more, *cara*."

"Time is such an invasion of privacy. Such a rude interruption," she droned, her voice heavy with disappointment.

"I have an upcoming exam. But would you like to meet at the lounge tomorrow night?" His spicy accent made it impossible to refuse anything he could ever ask of her.

"Of course. It's meant to be." The words were out before she realized she sounded dramatic. "I mean, there's no reason we shouldn't meet tomorrow."

"Nine is fine." A smile spread across his lips.

"Hey, you made a rhyme. That's cute." She returned his smile.

"My first ever in English. Maybe I should be a poet."

"You can write me a poem anytime." They stood and he helped her put her jacket on. "But your exam is more important. I can wait," she teased, making sure he knew it was a joke by giving him a wink. Then she mentally kicked herself—winks were a bit too forward for a first meeting. But she didn't put her foot in it by trying to explain that away.

She could have floated back up to her room without the elevator.

Of course, she Googled his name the second she got through the door. She checked Facebook and Twitter. He was one of many Antonio Calabreses in the world, but not under a Google search or on any social media sites.

He's serious about that studying, she thought as she Tweeted about what a fabulous trip she was having—minus the two murders.

The tourists gaped at Tutankhamen's preserved treasures: his bed, chariots, and personal items, such as sandals, jewelry, and gloves. They beheld the magnificent gold death mask. Anna Maria Russo left a bottle of tomato juice and a power bar in the corner as added provisions for the king's afterlife.

Antonio remained unhurt, yet Carmella watched his every move, praying for his safety and her own. But she couldn't quell that fear of some ancient curse on their tour guides. More realistically, somebody was out to get their guides. Somebody who didn't need any curse to succeed twice already.

Too stressed and jittery to return to her room, Carmella went to the hotel lounge after her parents retired for the night. She sat at the curved bar gazing at the picture she'd taken of Antonio with her cell phone earlier that day. She couldn't get him out of her mind. When the waiter came by, she ordered orange juice and noticed a well-dressed man checking her out, one seat away.

He ordered a drink. Under the dimly colored lights, his dark hair shone, radiating an aqua halo around his head. Dark brows shaded expressive eyes that missed nothing as they scanned the room and landed on her.

She wasn't interested in meeting anyone else—ever. Now that she'd finally found her life partner, she had no interest in even a Crown Prince.

He strode over and proffered the pleasure of his company.

"You're American, aren't you?" The hint of an alien tongue delicately accented his English.

"Yes, I am," she answered to be polite. "We're here on vaca—holiday."

"American girls bewitch me. You're so...free and easygoing."

"Easygoing I may be. Free I ain't," she muttered.

A gold medallion peeked out from under his open silk shirt, winking in the dim light against his mat of dark hair.

"I'm Hani Terif." His voice was smooth with a slight accent. "And you are?"

"Carmella Russo."

He leaned in. "Are you alone?" he stage-whispered.

She stared him in the eye and kept a straight face. "Not anymore. I'm engaged to be married. We're setting the date very soon."

"A-ha." He slipped a gold cigarette case out of his breast pocket and snapped it open, holding it out to her.

When he turned his head to speak to the bartender, she noticed a bandage above his ear. "No, thanks," she refused the offer of a long tapering cigarillo. "Smoking is a deadly vice."

"How about another drink, then?" He slid the case back into his pocket. "Drinks aren't deadly, if taken in moderation."

What harm in letting him buy her a glass of orange juice? "Fine. Orange juice, straight up."

She eyed his thick gold bracelet. "Gold is such a speculative commodity, isn't it?"

"Not when you're wearing it." His wide smile displayed more of the precious metal—a gold tooth directly behind his left canine. "I plan on bringing all my gold with me to the afterlife."

"Are you a Pharaoh?" she joked.

"Not quite," he answered, in all seriousness. "But I'd have to build a pyramid with a sixty-one-car garage."

Her brows shot up in surprise. "Sixty-one cars?"

"Only since I gave the two Bentleys away—to beautiful women like yourself."

"Thank you." She accepted the compliment with a smile, but the thought of a Bentley parked on her street made her laugh. "But a Bentley wouldn't fit in my neighborhood."

"I'm looking to give away a third. It's a law of the universe. That's one of the mysteries of the pyramids. Speaking of which, how about we take a ride past them? They're magnificent under illumination." He slid a wallet out of his pocket and took out a platinum American Express card.

"In one of your cars?" she asked, with no intention of going anywhere with him.

"Of course. What do you think we would take? A camel?" He chuckled as the bartender came by and took his card.

"Which one do you have tonight?"

"I was feeling sporty today." The bartender brought the slip back and he scribbled an illegible signature. It actually looked like hieroglyphics to her. "So, I brought one of the Ferraris out." He pointed out the floor-length window at a few cars parked under the portico. "There it is. I let the valet take it."

She looked out the window and saw a red sports car, sleek and low-slung. It probably cost more than her condo. "It's gorgeous. But one of the Ferraris, you said? How many do you have?" She swirled the ice cubes in her glass with the plastic stirrer. She couldn't decide if this guy was for real or just handing her a line.

"Oh, five or six. I lost count." He waved a dismissing hand as if telling her how many pairs of jeans he had. "But the one I have tonight, that's the new one. I bought it only last week. It's got impeccable security."

"You mean an extra loud alarm?" she asked.

He nodded. "That's only the beginning. It has bulletproof windows."

Her mouth fell open. She shut it.

"This is a dangerous place, my lady. And we've had more unrest than usual lately. A terrorist cell that calls themselves the Deadly Underground is active near here. Too near for my comfort. So, I had this car equipped." He lowered his head and pointed to the bandage she'd noticed earlier. "See this? I was driving with the windows open. Not a smart thing to do, especially in a car with bullet proof glass, but I wanted to catch the breeze. A hail of gunshot went off around me, and a bullet whizzed past, grazing my head."

Her mouth dropped open again. "Oh, God. Were you badly hurt?"

"No, it was just a graze. Nothing serious." He patted the spot as if he were proud of it.

"How did you keep from bleeding all over the inside of your Ferrari?"

He gave her a mysterious half-smile. "I did say my car was equipped. It has a first aid kit in the glove box. I pulled over and wrapped a bandage around my head and drove to the hospital. They patched me up quite well. Only needed a few stitches."

She gulped. "This is just so...foreign to me. I mean, we have drive-by shootings and homicides in the States, but here..." A jumble of emotions—anger, fear, outrage—riled her up. She grasped her glass and made a fist with her other hand. "I'm so thankful I don't live in the Middle East, in constant fear of suicide bombers." Her voice rose as the topic worked her up as it always did. "I lost friends on 9/11. Why can't the Israelis and Palestinians just get along and share the country and the religious sites instead of blowing each other to smithereens? It's crazy. If they all acted like you, they'd get along just fine."

His eyes narrowed and pierced her. "You don't know what it's like living like that every second of your life. You see it on the news, on the internet. But you have no idea—" He slammed his glass down and it shattered into pieces. Shards flew across the bar. He held up his bleeding hand.

She jumped to her feet, her nurturing instinct taking over. "I'll get you something..." She looked around but only saw skimpy cocktail napkins on the bar.

She ran through the lobby and up to the front desk. "Do you have any bandages?"

The polished clerk looked under the counter and shook her head. "Not right here. I can call for some. What room?"

"Never mind." She dashed outside as Hani Terif pointed out his Ferrari. The valet got out of a car parked in front of it.

"I have to get something out of the glove compartment," she said. With valet parking, the car was open.

She'd always wanted to ride in a Ferrari. She'd never even gotten close to one. She opened the passenger door and slid in. The sheepskin seat brushed against her bare legs like puffy clouds.

As she fumbled to open the glove compartment, she fingered its silver catch and its door fell open into her lap. She rifled through the compartment, rummaging through papers, finding a pair of designer sunglasses and a gold wristwatch. But no first aid kit.

Then she spotted an object that looked hauntingly familiar.

It was a Koran, bound in blue leather, the pages frayed at the edges where they'd been thumbed through many times. Where had she seen this before? Her mind rewound over the last few days and stopped short. Yasar! He carried a Koran identical to this one. He'd shown it to her and told her he'd got it at an auction.

An eerie warning made her skin crawl. She sensed something sinister about this book. She opened the inside cover, straining her eyes to read the print in the glove compartment's tiny circle of light. She clapped a hand over her mouth to stifle a scream. There, written in English, the name Yasar Massri, their first tour guide. How on earth did this Hani guy wind up with it, and what connection could he have with the dead tour guide? Had he also known Samir, the second victim?

Her heart lurched. She swallowed a lump of fear.

A credit card receipt marked a page in the center of the Koran. With trembling, sweaty hands, she opened to the marked page. Her eyes widened on some words scribbled in the margin, the language foreign to her. It could have been Hebrew, Farsi, or Aramaic, for all she knew. Fumbling and shaking, she ripped the scribbled page from the book and stuffed it into her skirt pocket.

She dashed back inside the hotel and to the lounge. Hani sat there, a bar towel wrapped around his hand. "I'm so sorry, I couldn't get a bandage." She didn't dare tell him where she'd looked. Before he got a word in edgewise, she blurted, "I hate to cut this short, but I do have to go. Nice meeting you." With a thousand pardons, she excused herself and fled the bar, half expecting a gunshot to make this moment her last.

She begged for Antonio's room number from the night clerk with a crisp $50 bill. She pounded on his door with her fist. Her heart could've banged on the door, it pounded so hard.

He opened his door, looking more tantalizing than ever in a pair of tight black sleeping shorts. The sight of him took her breath away. "Antonio, I'm sorry to wake you, but this is very important." She thrust the page at him. "What does this look like to you?"

He fanned his fingers though his tousled hair as he strained to decipher the mysterious scrawl. "Doesn't look familiar to me. As you Americans say, 'I don't dig.' Where did you get it?"

"I'll tell you later. You don't even know what language it is?"

"It's Arabic, but nothing within my limited vocabulary." He shook his head. "I can speak the language well enough, but the written words, I'm a very bad reader of the language."

She took it back from him with a shaking hand. "This means danger, I can feel it."

"Hey." He grasped her hand in his strong fingers and held it until she started to calm and breathe normally. "You're not in any harm. I won't let anything happen to you."

"Oh, Antonio, I'm so scared." She fell into his arms. "I know we shouldn't have taken this trip. They advised against it. This guy knows where we're staying. He's dangerous, I don't trust him!"

"What guy?"

She took a ragged breath, trembling once again. "This guy Hani I met in the lounge. We started to talk..." She told him what happened.

He smoothed her hair and walked her to the bed. Sitting her down, he grabbed a tissue and dabbed at the tears that ran in streaks down her face. "You're not in danger, *cara*. He won't harm you. You're perfectly safe. Just enjoy your time in Egypt and don't even think about danger."

She gulped several times and caught her breath. As the initial shock wore off, she thought more clearly. "I don't want anything to happen to you, either. Our last two tour guides were murdered. Why aren't you frantic over that?" Through her tears, his blurred image came into focus as she blinked.

He inched closer to her and raised her chin with his fingertip. "Because I'm not involved in any political group or do anything that terrorists or anyone else would consider a target. I mind my own business and stay out of politics or causes or issues that get people killed here. I don't talk about politics with my friends or family. I don't even want to talk about it with you."

She inhaled and exhaled as if in Yoga class. Her heart slowed to its normal rate. Relief flooded her. She slid her jacket off and placed it beside her. "You don't have to tell me your political leanings. I don't really have any myself. I'm middle of the road all the way. Not one extreme or the other about anything. I even vote Libertarian." She covered her mouth. "Oops, we're not supposed to talk about it." They shared a moment of much-needed levity with a laugh.

"Well, you have nothing to worry about. You're safe, and I certainly am." He stood and opened the minibar. "Those other guides must have been involved with some group and caused trouble or said the wrong thing to the wrong person." He took out two tiny wine bottles and twisted the caps off. "Some people don't know when to keep their mouths shut." He poured the wine into two glasses and brought them over. "Here. It's not Italy's finest vintage, but it will do for now." They clinked the glasses and he raised his to his lips.

"Wait." She grasped his glass. "I want to make a toast. To us. To the first day of our future together. We both know what's happening here. And although our bodies never met in this life, our souls definitely have in some other life, maybe centuries ago. We belong together, Antonio. A miracle brought me here. I was supposed to die in that plane crash. But instead, I'm here with you. I defied all odds getting here, and so did you. We were meant to meet and be together. You can't deny that, can you?"

He touched his glass to hers once more and gazed into her eyes, holding that gaze until she nearly drowned in his adoration of her. "No, I cannot deny it. It is a miracle that we're both here. It's meant to be. And that's *amore*."

She entered her hotel room an hour later and gasped in disbelief. The room was in a shambles; the furniture overturned, the mattress on its side against the wall, the curtains torn from their rods, her clothes and personal belongings strewn about as if a cyclone had hit the room. The carpet was yanked up at the edges. Her emptied shampoo bottles lay scattered on the bathroom floor.

As she stood, numb with shock, the closet door hit her in the rear. A clammy hand clapped over her mouth. A cold hard gun barrel pressed against her neck. She shivered as sweat soaked her back.

"Too bad such a lovely lady is such a snoop," said the same velvety voice that had complimented American girls on their free spiritedness and bragged about sixty-one cars. But now it sent a quiver of terror down her spine. "We're going for a ride, but not to King Tut's tomb. It's going to be to yours. If you don't cooperate."

He removed his hand. She gasped for breath. "No, Hani—"

With nothing to guide her but basic survival instinct, she let out a piercing scream and bit down on his hand.

He struck her with his pistol. A blinding flash of pain seared her skull as she collapsed to the floor.

Awakening, on the edge of awareness, her first sensation was the searing heat of the night and the pressure against her stomach. As her eyes slid open, she saw the hotel's stairwell. Her head throbbed. Sweat drenched her body. Again, she blacked out.

Reality flooded back. She stood on a desolate road. Dazed,

she kept telling herself *I'm dreaming. I've had nightmares before. I'm dreaming; I know it.*

Mouth shut, she obediently walked alongside her captor, over the unpaved road. They stopped at a Ferrari parked in a narrow alley. She recognized it as his as he shoved her and sent her sprawling to the dirt.

This is no dream, she realized as sheer terror stabbed her heart.

"Where is it?" he growled.

"Where is what?" She frantically searched her clouded mind for a bluff.

"The page you ripped out of the Koran. You know damn well what!"

"I—gave it to the police. Just before I came up to my room. They're going to be here any second!" Her words ran together in a slur. Her heart pounded like thunder.

"Listen, bitch. I would be the prisoner instead of you if you'd given it to the police. Now where is it?" He shoved the pistol between her breasts while pinning her to the ground with his free arm, his gold medallion dangling in her face. She smelled his pungent sweat mingled with an exotic cologne. "Turn out your pockets. I know it's on you. Out with it."

Weary with fright and defeat, she reached down and retrieved the flimsy page from her pocket. He grabbed it.

"Goodbye," he rasped. "Perhaps we'll meet again in that great pyramid—in the sky." He let out a sinister laugh as he aimed his automatic at her, prolonging her agony.

She lay cringing, eyes tightly shut, waiting for pain, darkness, the afterworld. But nothing came. She opened her eyes but Hani still stood above her, the gun aimed at her chest. Her eyes widened as she spotted a shadowy figure crouched behind her would-be murderer.

She gasped. *Antonio!*

To cover her surprise, as well as buy time for her rescuer, she accused, "So it was you who killed Yasar!"

Hani replied, "Yes, and your other tour guide, too, and several Israeli soldiers when I escaped the Bishara farmhouse. I was the only member of the Deadly Underground to survive," he bragged.

Antonio crept forward in silence, now within ten feet of Hani. *Think fast!* Carmella demanded of her still-foggy mind. "Can I make up my face? I wouldn't want anyone to find me like this!" she babbled, her eyes darting toward Antonio's silhouette, a short eternity from saving her.

Confusion flitted across Hani's face; his brows knitted, his lips spread in a dumb sneer.

Antonio sprang from the shadows and leapt on Hani's back. Hani whirled to shake off his attacker, but a heartbeat later, shot at Carmella.

The moment's hesitation saved her life. The gun roared, but the shot went wide of its mark. The jarring thud of Antonio's tackle diverted Hani's aim from its target.

Carmella lay paralyzed with fear and a dread fascination as the muscular bodies struggled on the ground, slippery and glowing with sweat. Another shot fired. Its brilliant flash showed the men grasping for the gun, for life itself. A grunt, a third shot, silence. It was over. Both men lay still as death.

She sprang to her feet and rushed to Antonio's prone body, searching his neck for a pulse as she lifted his head onto her lap.

Antonio opened his eyes and asked one question: "Are you all right?"

"Yes! Are you?"

"I'm slightly wounded," He clutched his shoulder and winced. "But he's—I think I got him worse." He propped himself up on his elbows and brushed dirt from his pants legs.

Straining to see in the darkness, she looked over at Hani.

His sightless eyes stared straight ahead. A stream of blood trailed from his gaping mouth. "He's not moving. It doesn't look like he's breathing either."

"Then he's already at the pearly gates." Antonio struggled to stand but she nudged him back.

"No, don't stand up. I'll call for an ambulance." She gulped the hot desert air as she took a breath. "How did you know to come here?"

"I was on my way back to your room to return your jacket that you'd left in my room. I heard you scream and followed you here. That writing...it seems to be important. You must take it to the police, show them the list. I can't go with you. I've been hit. I don't think I should move until a doctor gets here. Take my cell phone from my jacket pocket and call five-one-zero. That's the emergency number."

"Yes, please be okay..." she whispered, tenderly lowering his head to the sand-strewn ground. His eyes closed as she fished his phone from his pocket. Wiping her sweaty palm on her blouse, she punched out the number and held the phone to his ear. He rattled off a quick sentence in Arabic and nodded to her.

She tiptoed towards the terrorist's lifeless body, dipped two fingers into his pocket, and slid out the frayed, crumpled paper that had cost so many lives. She slid that precious item between her breasts.

An ambulance screeched up to them and rushed them to the hospital. She sat with Antonio in the ambulance, clasping his hand, her eyes glued to the erratic blip that monitored his heartbeat.

U.S. Ambassador Carl Wilson entered the hospital room where Antonio sat up drinking coffee. Carmella watched him through every minute of his recovery, falling more and more deeply in love with the real-live hero she'd always waited for and dreamed of.

The Ambassador removed his hat and smiled down at the courageous couple.

"Young man, and young lady," the Ambassador addressed each in turn, "not only are you lucky to be alive, but you're both heroes. The United States of America owes you a great deal for helping to prevent a massacre. We knew the Deadly Underground were about to strike, but we didn't know where. You've saved the lives of seven Israeli members of Parliament and a delegation to the U.N. That list you gave us was the Deadly Underground's hit list. We owe you both, and I hope you'll let us know if there's anything we can do for yourselves or your families."

Antonio looked at his new fiancée and took her hand. "Well, Signor, there is something you can do for my family, since I'm acquiring a new one very soon. This is my wife-to-be Carmella. Her lifelong dream is to marry an Italian in Italy and bring him back home, as her great-grandparents did. Only this marriage is anything but arranged."

"Oh, it was arranged, all right," Carmella corrected him, beaming at the Ambassador. "The universe arranged it, many years ago when I first put out my request. Now that my wish has been granted, I want to show my thanks. So, I'm inviting you and a guest to our wedding, which I've always dreamed would be in the Sistine Chapel. And to accept your offer to help..." She cast Antonio a loving gaze. "I know weddings aren't allowed there, they don't even allow photos, but neither of us has any Vatican connections. Any chance you can use your influence to let a small—say, no more than a dozen—wedding guests into the chapel?"

Ambassador Wilson's eyes darted about as he considered the proposition. "Hmmm, that's a tall order. I can't promise anything, but once the folks at the Vatican hear your story, how could they refuse? I know Michelangelo would want to see you exchange vows surrounded by his exquisite works of art. I also know what romantics Italians are. But it might not be tomorrow. Rome wasn't built in a day, you know."

"Of course, Signor," Antonio answered for them both. "The Sistine Chapel waited five hundred years for us, we certainly can wait a short while for it."

The flight back to London left precisely on schedule. Back in coach sat Professor Everett, typing notes on his laptop, Janice Everett admiring her new turquoise rosary beads, and Jeff Sullivan designing a new computer game, "Ramses's Revenge."

In the center row sat Anna Maria Russo, studying the diagram of the aircraft's emergency exits, and Carmella sat in the aisle seat. Antonio sat next to her.

As the plane reached cruising altitude, Carmella pushed her seat back and reclined. A man walked down the aisle, flipping through the pages of a small blue book. He dropped it directly at her side, and as he bent over to pick it up, she espied the cover. That imitation leather, that gold lettering, the frayed pages...

A wave of sick panic invaded her. Grabbing Antonio's arm, she groped for words, unable to form a coherent sentence.

"It's—it's the blue Koran. He's got it!" Carmella gasped, her heart in her throat.

Antonio chuckled, cupping her cheek. "It's nothing to

worry about. We're perfectly safe, nothing's going to happen to us." He kissed her softly, then reached into his pocket.

He pulled out a small blue leather Koran and flipped to the center, revealing the frayed gap where that deadly page had been torn out. "You see," he said, "I acquired a little souvenir of my own."

BOG BODIES

THE EMACIATED man lay on his side in the fetal position. His leathery bronzed skin cast a dull glow in the waning sunlight. Besides a brown leather cap and belt, he wore nothing. But he was hardly a nude sunbather out here in the peat bog with only two accessories to complement his birthday suit.

He was a two-thousand-year-old corpse.

"It's uncanny. He looks like he could have died yesterday." The archaeology student shook his head in wonder as his mentor, Professor Wilhelm Jorgensen, and five other students stared down at the perfectly preserved body.

Professor Jorgensen rose from his kneeling position at the edge of the shallow grave, swept his glasses off and turned to the amazed students. Thrusting his hands deeper into his pockets to shield them against the whipping Danish wind, he explained, "This is one of many, my friends. More than a hundred of these bodies have been found in peat bogs here in Tollund Fen, as well as Northern Germany and the Netherlands. The peat stained him, and its iron-bearing acids preserved him. Examination of nearby pollen tells us that these burials took place about two thousand years ago."

Geir Svenning stepped away from his fellow students, all tapping away on their tablets. He stood over the grave, his blond hair flying in all directions, his zealous gaze fixed on the dead man's placid expression. The head, embedded in the ground at a three-quarter profile, exposed heavy eyelids and a slim aquiline nose, the lips parted to reveal yellowed teeth. Tufts of dusty hair sprinkled the skin stretched over the skull. An exposed arm bone jutted from the remaining flesh at a right angle to the drawn-up knees. Geir anticipated the feel of the ancient flesh under his sensitive fingerpads. "What are we going to do with him, Professor?" Geir dug into his pocket for his reliable roll of antacids.

"Excavators from the National Museum are going to crate him and ship him off to Copenhagen to study him. With their permission, we'll be able to audit the investigation and find out more about this mysterious old chap." He snapped a few photos of the corpse with his cell phone. "Until they give him a proper name, we'll call him Tollund Man."

At the Copenhagen museum, a team of archaeologists made another shattering discovery while examining Tollund Man. On removing a lump of peat from beside the head, they found a leather noose pulled tightly around the man's neck. As Geir and Professor Jorgensen stood by observing, one astonished face met the other as the puzzle snapped together: Tollund Man had been strangled.

Geir turned the page of his yellowing journal. It was twenty years to the day since he'd begun recording entries. The feel of the leafy pages instantly brought him back to that day when he extended his right hand to touch the ancient brow. Surprisingly, it hadn't felt like leather. It was hard and smooth, fossilized, like the sandals he'd excavated from a vanished town in Northern Iraq, dating back to 1500 B.C.

Returning to the journal, he reviewed his scrawled notes of Professor Jorgensen's lecture after they'd determined the reason of Tollund Man's death: he had been quietly slain and offered to the gods at a Nordic pagan ritual. He could have been a priest, or simply a martyr, relinquishing his earthly life for his survivors. His last meal, upon investigation of his digestive tract, had been grains and sunflower seeds, ingested to germinate and grow by the goddess's journey through the spring landscape. *Sunflower seeds!* Geir marveled. *Still intact and undigested after two thousand years!*

He shut his eyes as the image from twenty centuries ago appeared in his mind.

"Geeeir!" His wife's piercing shriek shattered his thoughts and sent him crashing back to Earth; to his life as an overworked archaeology professor and to his tragically unhappy marriage. Gudrun would undoubtedly demand that he carry out another menial chore: take out the trash or wash his coffee cup or search for the remote she'd misplaced.

He found her lounging on the living room sofa, painting her fingernails a piercing blood red, a grotesque contrast to her orange tunic and canary yellow hair. "Make me a snack, dearie, I've been so busy all day shopping, standing in long lines, my shoes nearly choking my feet..." She stretched and yawned. "I'll make it up to you. I'll fix you dinner one night next week."

Geir wouldn't have minded so much if she just wanted to lounge around the house, reading magazines and playing on the internet. Eager to give her everything he could afford, he'd hired a maid and a cook. But all she'd produced in a decade and a half of marriage were two meals burned beyond recognition, on their first and tenth anniversaries. Her incessant demands and whining pleas for more money made her unbearable to live with.

"Why not divorce her?" his colleagues, aware of his plight, repeatedly asked him.

"Simple," he'd reply. "I cannot afford it." He was in more than a rut, he was in a grave; a catacomb deep within Mother Earth from which no mortal man could escape. Just like the sacrificial Tollund Man he'd examined twenty years ago. Strangled, dumped into a grave, a sacrifice to the gods, a sacrifice, a sacrifice...

The word whistled through his mind like a musical phrase as he poured a mixture of seeds and nuts into a bowl. How much would Gudrun really be willing to sacrifice? Would she ever sacrifice anything for this marriage...or for its merciful end?

Professor Jorgensen's words echoed over two decades: "Who killed this man two thousand years ago?" The professor had put the rhetorical question to the class, thirty eager junior archaeologists, each wanting to make that one discovery that would herald their success. "Two thousand years and we'll never know."

"They'll never know," Geir repeated Professor Jorgensen's words out loud, echoing the deep intrusive voice, the tone he always tried to emulate while lecturing his own students. Trying to still his trembling hands, he placed the bowl of seeds and nuts on the table in front of his wife.

"What are you mumbling about?" Gudrun demanded, twisting the bottle cap closed as the pungent odor of nail polish dissolved into the air.

"Nothing, nothing. You keep on doing...whatever it is you do." He exited the living room and headed for Gudrun's walk-in closet. He snapped on the light and before his eyes appeared a wardrobe to rival a top fashion model. He scanned the array of colorful garments: flowered frocks, cashmere sweaters, leather trousers, all boasting designer labels. He saw a stack of hats about to topple from the shelf above; handbags every color of the rainbow hung from hooks on the far wall. Plastic compartments at his feet held enough footwear to shoe a family of centipedes. His eyes roamed a bit farther, to the opposite corner, where she stored her accessories. All genuine leather, nothing but the best. How many alligators, lambs, and elks had sacrificed their hides to clothe Gudrun Svenning in elegant splendor? More shoes, belts, and handbags studded and trimmed with gleaming gold hardware. He extended an arm and flipped through the leather straps hanging from a revolving belt-tree. The buckles tinkled gently as they clinked against one another, brown belts, red belts, so many belts.

No one will ever know.

"You're right, Professor," Geir replied to the twenty-year-old lament. "No one ever will."

Geir's clicking heels echoed through the dark hall as he approached the research laboratory. Shining his flashlight on the lock, he inserted the key and leaned on the heavy door. It groaned on its rusty hinges as he stepped inside, opened the glass case with a smaller key, and retrieved the one item he needed. Stuffing it into his pocket, he replaced it with one of his own and shut the glass case. He then lifted a bottle of concentrated sulfuric acid off a high shelf, taking pains to ensure that the deadly liquid wouldn't escape the rubber stopper. He popped an antacid into his mouth as he exited the lab, locked up, and returned to his car.

He grasped her wrist between his thumb and forefinger to make sure she was dead. The ancient leather noose had nearly snapped but he'd pulled as tightly as his strength would allow as he watched his wife's last breath depart the thrashing body. The lips paled to blue as color abandoned the cheeks, fading to a chalky marble. Another pagan ritual—however, a very modern one.

He removed her clothes, tossing aside the silk housecoat, yanking the ermine slippers from the icy feet. The sun had sunk; darkness enshrouded the room. His eyes adjusted to the pitchy shadows as he wiped the red polish from her fingernails with a cotton swab and a bottle of remover he'd found on her vanity table among the serums and creams.

His odometer indicated he was 56 kilometers from Aarhus. He pulled over next to a peat bog similar to the one in which they'd found Tollund Man. He dug a four-foot grave and sprinkled pollen seeds around its edges. Working in the muted beams of his car's headlamps, he flexed his gloved hands, dragged his wife's body from the car and stained the skin brown with the peat. Arranging it into a fetal position, he dumped it into the grave, the noose tightly bound about the neck. He poured acid over the hands and face to emulate quick decomposition and obliterate her facial features and fingerprints. He shoveled the peat back into the grave.

The simple ritual completed, he dashed back to his car,

tossed the shovel into the back seat and drove away, munching on sunflower seeds.

Now Gudrun belonged to the gods—a Tollund Woman.

~

"Yes, Inspector, she's been gone over two weeks. I bought her a train ticket to Copenhagen, just to get her out of the house. I neglected her terribly. I've been so busy the last few weeks."

Inspector Larsen nodded, chewing on his overgrown mustache with a busy lower lip. "Did you check with the Copenhagen police?"

"Yes, several times. There's been no sign of her." Geir forced anguish into his tone and wrung his hands.

The Inspector pushed past Geir towards the bedroom and scanned the area. Geir guided him over to Gudrun's closet, flipped the switch, and let the Inspector thumb through the clothes. His huge paws grabbed at dresses, jackets, and trousers.

"She hasn't taken much with her, has she?" The Inspector turned to Geir, still wringing his hands, trying to force tears.

Geir fumbled for words, his hair falling into his eyes as he picked up Gudrun's silver comb and swept the unruly strands from his forehead. "Well, she's...she's always had lots of clothes, you know...you know women..." he emitted a little chuckle. The Inspector didn't join him. Instead, he turned and walked towards Gudrun's vanity, exactly as she had left it. He contemplated the array of cosmetics with a speck of wonder in his eye. He scrutinized one item at a time, perusing the numerous bottles of nail polish: Copper Frost, Cosmic Crimson, Sky Blue Pink. "That's some shade of red," he commented on the Cosmic Crimson. He abandoned the nail polishes and studied the eye shadows, the face powders, all bearing descriptive shades: Tawny Peach, Barely Beige, Blushing Pink. "A woman who wears this much makeup shouldn't be very hard to find," he remarked.

"She just had no reason to leave. None at all. We were so happy together," Geir emphasized that last sentence.

"She really had it made, huh?" One thick eyebrow shot up and disappeared under the shadow of the Inspector's hat as he turned to exit Gudrun's powder room.

"She had just about everything a woman could want," Geir insisted, shaking his head. "I miss her terribly."

"I'm sure you do." The Inspector regarded the antique furnishings, the silk Turkish rug. After recording more information in his notepad, he assured Geir he'd be in touch and turned to leave. Geir saw him out and popped an antacid into his mouth.

With a spark of *déjà vu* igniting his memory, Professor Geir Svenning answered a summons to the phone while lecturing. A body recently discovered near Aarhus...workmen cutting peat had found it...this was a female...similar to all the others...

Would he like to see it?

He saw Inspector Larsen at the site with several students peering into the grave, displaying wide-eyed gaping-mouthed astonishment.

"What's your opinion on this, Professor?" The Inspector greeted him, his finger on the button of a small digital recorder. Two students approached Geir and clicked on their recorders, thrusting them into his face.

"It's...it's another of the sacrificial pagans..." he began, only having glanced briefly into the three-year-old grave at the woman, the leather noose intact as the night he'd fastened it.

"This woman lived during northern Europe's Iron Age, at the beginning of the Christian era."

He concluded his statement with Professor Jorgensen's famous axiom: "But no one will ever know." He added, chuckling, "Our good Inspector here was probably still walking the beat when this crime took place. You're wasting your time trying to solve this case, sir. Leave this one to us archaeologists."

The Inspector motioned for the students to move on. They wandered away after one last glimpse into the grave, unable to conceal their shared grimaces and smirks.

"It's very interesting, Professor. Thank you for enlightening us." The Inspector held out a calloused hand and Geir took it. They shook.

"You're very welcome, Inspector. Now I must be going, I've got a class at eleven." He smiled, taking his time turning and heading for his car, wiping the beads of sweat off his upper lip.

"Just one last item, Professor Svenning." The Inspector's voice rang through his ears like the clap of the doomsday bell.

"What is it?" He stopped and turned halfway, fighting to keep the tension out of his voice as his heart began to slam.

"You've overlooked one minor detail in your cursory examination of this Iron Age woman, Professor. Two-thousand-year-old pagans did not put Cosmic Crimson polish on their toenails."

HIS OWN BOSS

New York City, 1933

Rookie cop Jimmy DeBari approached Lieutenant Frank Russo as the ambulance hauled the latest victim off to the morgue.

"Lieutenant, Sir, I don't know how you did it," DeBari gushed. "But I certainly hope I can crack a case this big someday."

"You will, son, you certainly will." Frank hiked his holster up against his hip. "By the time you're in my position, murders like this'll be small potatoes. Maybe you'll bust up a syndicate. That'll be something to tell your grandchildren about."

"As long as I can tell them I knew you, sir, that's enough for me!" DeBari smiled.

Frank turned to the imposing Captain George Murphy. "I've done all I can do down here, Murph. I'm going home to catch the last half of Amos 'N Andy."

"Yeah, Frank, just go on home." Captain Murphy regarded the young lieutenant with his mussel-shell eyes and crossed the room of the bullet-ridden haberdashery, barely betraying the limp he'd acquired after being wounded in the Great War. "Someday..." he muttered to himself, fingering his cold badge. "Someday..."

Frank strode up the porch steps of his three-story walk-up and entered the narrow hall that always smelled of lye and garlic. *Another murder case cracked,* he thought with a smug grin, and another feather in the cap of the youngest lieutenant on the Jersey City Police Force. At thirty, he'd already clamped down on the source of one of the city's oldest loan-sharking operations, the powerful Lionetti family. He'd sent an army of *compari* and hangers-on to prison for life. He had ways, he had methods, and he had sources—but most of all he had two tightly clamped lips that opened only to heaping pasta dishes and his father's homemade red wine.

Frank entered his four-room rear apartment and opened the window that looked out over an air shaft. "Gotta get outta this dump," he muttered, slapping together a bologna sandwich. He headed for the Zenith radio and fiddled with the buttons.

Capo Antonio Lionetti, or "Boss Tony" to his small army of soldiers and "button men", seethed through clenched teeth. After his apprenticeship in Detroit's notorious Purple Gang, he'd finally attained his present pinnacle of power. From a lowly button man, he rose through the ranks, proving to the old "Mustache Petes" that he was capable of a murderous proficiency in the art of contract killing, settling labor union disputes by breaking limbs with almost surgical precision, and by hurling bombs through noncompliant store owners' windows.

All his hard work was now in danger of being nullified. Glancing once more at the newspaper's glaring headline, he pounded his fist on the table. The ashtray flipped over as puffs of ash and chomped cigar ends showered the room, spattering his pin-striped suit.

"Again! He did it again!" Cursing under his breath, he lunged for the telephone and dialed Captain Murphy. Two rings, then three. "Where is that buffoon?" he growled, as Murphy's sleepy voice replaced the monotonous ringing.

"You," Boss Tony rasped. "How'd Russo get away wit' it, willya tell me? He just knocked off one of our best men! What's goin' on here, buster, ain't you doin' your jobs?"

"I don't know, Boss. God help me, I don't know. Russo won't tell us how he cracked that case or any of the others. His lips are sealed."

"Yeah, well the rest of him's gonna be sealed in a concrete suit unless you quit screwin' around and find out how this guy gets all the dirt on us. I can cut you off just as easy as I can cut a rump roast in half!" He slammed the handset down, leaving a stunned Captain Murphy to agonize, for the dozenth time, over how Frank Russo exposed all their nefarious operations.

"Ah, dumb luck, it's gotta be," Murphy mumbled. Satisfied enough with his theory, he rolled over to catch up on the sleep he'd lost.

Settled in his office chair at Mulberry Street Police Headquarters, Frank Russo grabbed the jangling telephone.

"Hey, Russo," The voice was as familiar as his own mother's echoing down Mott Street for him to come home to eat. The faceless, enigmatic voice that would speak to no one on the force but him. The voice that everyone knew was his source, and who would rather see Armageddon than reveal its identity.

"Yeah, whatcha got this time?" Frank caused all heads to turn towards him as propped his feet up on the chipped wooden desk.

"One person that doesn't have to drink bathtub gin is Boss Lionetti," the voice continued, smooth as a shot of smooth Scotch trickling down a dry throat. "He's been bootlegging since before Prohibition, for the practice."

"Is that right?" Russo urged, nodding. The other cops gathered around him in anticipation of the next prophecy. "And what pray tell can we do about this illicit operation?"

"He's got a big shipment due at the foot of Montgomery Street at two tomorrow morning. A few thousand gallons of hooch, due for delivery to all his trusty distributors. Now we all know bootlegging's against the law of this great land, don't we, Russo?"

"Well, everybody's gotta have a hobby. Thanks, pal. After this, Lionetti'll wish he'd taken up flagpole sitting." He replaced the handset and met the eyes of his squad members, one pair at a time, each wider and more agog than the next.

"You guys go home and get some sleep. Then we're all meeting at the foot of Montgomery Street at two in the morning. Sharp. And you're gonna see history repeat itself because we've been invited to a reenactment of the Boston Tea Party, Jersey style!"

The last thing Boss Lionetti expected was for that peach-fuzz-faced Russo to close down his bootlegging operation after all this time.

"'The world's gonna come crashin' down on this city if we don't take action," he spoke calmly to Captain Murphy, so calmly it scared him. Why didn't he shout and pound his fists like he always did? That he could handle. But when Boss

Lionetti spoke so calmly and carefully, his cigar wedged between the thick lips as he spoke, Murphy narrowed his eyes, wary. So, he ad-libbed it with what he considered a brainstorm: "I've got it, Boss. We'll set up a phony job. Lionetti'll head on down to the scene, and nothin'll ruin the delivery tonight. We'll send him clear across the precinct, down to that Polish section if you want."

"Are you kiddin'?" Boss Tony scowled. "Down there they consider it a crime if some housewife don't scrub her porch clean enough. Send him to Bart's Jewelry Store. Tell him there's gonna be a heist and he's gotta cover it with his silver shiny badge and his forty-five rod."

Murphy splayed his fingers. "And then when he gets down there, what are the owners s'posed to do when he starts shooting now and asking questions later?"

"Nuttin'." Boss Tony smirked. "They'll be too busy playin' poker in the back room to even know he's there."

But the silky-smooth voice told Frank Russo where to be. He arrived, did his job, and once again stunned all but the crew in the back room of Bart's Jewelry Store, whose all-night poker game continued uninterrupted.

"Get rid of 'im," Boss Tony demanded. "Enough is enough. I've been a nice guy too long. You don't get rid of 'im, I will."

Captain Murphy watched in stunned silence as Boss Tony chomped on the cigar between his stained teeth. "I'm convinced he's got a source. Doing away with him won't solve nothing, Boss. We've got to find his source. That's who we waste, not him. I can send him packing and we'll never hear from him again. The boys down at the station keep telling me he gets these anonymous tipoffs: these brief, one-minute conversations, just snatches of dialogue, almost in code like, and Russo follows up on it. But that's where I'm stumped. Who can it be?"

Boss Tony shook his head. "I dunno. But I ain't gonna waste time playin' Charlie Chan. I'll give you twenty-four hours. I'll get my boys on it, too." His eyes glared at the captain like two eight balls, the dull yellowish whites matching his teeth like wardrobe accessories.

"Sure, Boss. I'll get right on it." Murphy respectfully bowed his head and vanished.

Boss Tony's stepdaughter Anna Maria approached him and divulged her feelings for the man who'd captured her heart. His name was Frank Russo. "He's so strong and handsome. He has black wavy hair and broad shoulders, smooth cheekbones, bright green eyes, and he dresses so well..."

Tony removed his cigar for the first time since eight o'clock that morning. Leaning forward, he extended his arm and delivered a blow that sent Maria reeling across the room to crash into the far wall, her hands spread protectively across her bruised face. "You stupid girl!" he exploded, looking past her out the window, his eyes fixed on a scraggly tree that bore a grotesque resemblance to his stepdaughter as she cowered against the wall. "Don't you see what he's trying to do! He wants to control my empire and now he's ruining your reputation, employing you as a pipeline to my affairs! Get outta here! Now!"

Anna Maria sidestepped out of the room, heaving a ragged sob as she reached the doorway.

"And if you mention Frank Russo's name again, I'll put you in the convent!"

∼

The voice sounded a bit ruffled, yet still retained its flowing cadence.

"They're onto you, baby. They know you've got a source and they're trying to crack us. Now what do we do?"

"Just the opposite of what they expect us to do. Nothing." Frank Russo polished a gold cufflink and inserted it into the buttonhole of his sleeve, cradling the handset between his neck and shoulder. "Just tell me if you know of anything that's going on tonight."

"Well, yes, as a matter of fact, I do. Dom's Tavern is the place to be tonight. Mayor Craig is going to accept a handsome kickback from the Scarlatti contractor for that new school. Tonight, between seven and nine. You know his silver-trimmed Duesenberg, don't you?"

"Sure do. The mayor, huh? I gotta be there. I just can't sit back and watch my city fall prey to the hands of a corrupt leader. Just tell the press to get out those big block letters they use for extra big headlines. See you on Page One."

The squad watched their leader. The two words "Mayor Craig" were all they had to hear. Stunned, they listened while the lieutenant told them that he'd be able to crack this one himself. This was going to be a very clean one, and easy, too.

∼

Jersey City was preparing for a new mayoral election and Boss Tony's fists clenched tightly enough to crush a sewer rat into oblivion.

"Your twenty-four hours was up a long time ago, pal!" he exploded at Captain Murphy. "The cement mixer's all ready to make him a right turn onto Railroad Avenue. And I ain't wastin' any more time. He's ruinin' us, ya *gavone*."

"Take it easy, Boss," Captain Murphy tried to appease Boss Tony with his Colgate tooth powder smile. "I've got good news. You're gonna love it. I fired Russo yesterday. Threw him out on his ear. He's takin' off to Florida. We got nothin' to worry about no more. Now, how about we get the ferry across the river and go to Umberto's for some manicotti to celebrate? I'll treat."

Obviously pleased, Boss Tony smiled, the light shining on his balding pate like a beacon. "Buono, buono. But we go to Calabrese's. Don't worry about payin' no bill there."

"Oh, I must treat you, Boss." Murphy clasped his hands together.

"I never pay at Calabrese's." He brandished a smug smirk.

"You know the owner then?" Murphy's eyes bugged out.

"Yeah, real well." He cocked a bushy brow. "You're lookin' at 'im, stupido!"

Before Frank Russo tucked his train ticket to Miami into his inner jacket pocket, he sent an anonymous mass card to Boss Tony's family for a good reason—the man would be dead within twelve hours.

"Calabrese's," the voice had said. "For dinner."

He didn't have to be there. Someone would do the job on his behalf. Now that nearly all of Boss Tony's operations were in check, it was time to do away with the patriarch of that inexcusably corrupt family once and for all. He'd wait until after dinner—let the man enjoy his last dish of manicotti—and then it would all be over. Another "Mustache Pete" gone.

He went down to the incinerator and tossed a package onto the coals. The package contained his policeman's uniform.

He went out to the backyard and held a symbolic burial service for his silver badge, which had tarnished a bit around the edges. He dug a hole and placed it in its grave, uttering a eulogy for the doomed police force. "Without me, they'll surely fall apart." He brushed the dirt particles off his hands and headed back inside to finish packing.

His phone call came at precisely two minutes past eight. Boss Tony should have been dead for two minutes now.

"It's all done," the voice came through brimming with self-satisfaction.

"He full of holes?" Frank asked, his lips spreading in a grin.

"Like Swiss cheese."

"Good." He smirked in satisfaction.

"It's all smooth sailing now, we're all waiting for you to step in and take over...Boss Frank."

"Thank you, Anna Maria. But first we're going to Miami for a nice well-deserved vacation."

"I HAVE OTHER PLANS..."

"With your personality and my brains, we'll make a fortune. How can we lose? This is Houston!" Ben Blanchard gushed to Roy White with a sweeping gesture at the elegant Galleria complex across from Roy's plush office. "I'll do all the marketing, you do all the technical work, and we'll be rolling in it before you can lasso an armadillo. Face it, Roy. You need me. And I can whip this business into shape faster than you can jump your next plane to Cancun. How 'bout it, then? Forty-nine per cent of the shares. Is it a deal? I'll pay for myself many times over."

Roy fingered his stiffened monogrammed cuffs and fiddled with his 'executive toy,' five clicking balls suspended from strings, marvelously adhered to the laws of physics. "Tell you what, Ben," he began, his tone low and monotonous. "I'll give you ten per cent of the fees. That should work out to about half of the profits—sometimes more, sometimes less. I just can't give you that much stock. I've got three stockholders as it is and..." He took a deep breath. "I can't take a step like that now." He turned his aging eyes to the energetic go-getter, seeing the raw eagerness. Roy knew the kid was a dynamo. He also knew enough thirty-five-year-olds thumbing it across the country without the vaguest idea of what a tax return looked like. His son was one of them.

"I understand." Ben nodded. "A tenth of the profits is perfectly acceptable." He folded his arms across his chest. "But you can't do all the marketing as well as all the work, too, Roy. You're killing yourself. You need—"

"All right, Ben." Roy held his hand up. "You delivered your sales pitch and I bit. Now quit babbling about how great you are and go out and produce."

Ben raised his right hand to his brow in a mock salute. "Ay ay, sir. But before I set the world on fire, how's about one last three-martini lunch for the road?"

So began the partnership known to the business world as White Enterprises, LLC. In four short years, the charming, dynamic, and dressed-for-success Ben Blanchard had quadrupled the company's gross sales, making them one of Houston's top 500 businesses. The hefty profits brought sprawling houses, flashy cars, jaunts to Tahiti, and a full-color spread in Texas Monthly.

But Ben Blanchard still owned a mere ten per cent of the company he'd singlehandedly resurrected. "Let's go public," he'd suggested to Roy one day while in flight to San Antonio to inspect a construction site.

"Not on your life!" Roy, who'd recently bought out his three other partners, chomped on peanuts.

Disappointed, Ben shrugged, turned away to gaze out the window, and continued to live with his ten per cent.

Until his wife started badgering him.

"For God's sakes, Ben, can't you see what he's doing to you? You're no more than a go-fer who goes running all over town in this sticky heat, sitting in traffic, taking his cronies to power lunches. He hires more peons to do his work while he sits on his butt reading the Wall Street Journal and reaping his ninety per cent. After you build him a solid enough client base, he's going to squeeze that ten out of you just like he did with his other partners. He wants it all for himself. And we'll be out on the street with nothing to show for it."

"Roy would never do a thing like that, Sybil," Ben argued back, checking his trousers carefully for hanging threads. "Besides, he's no good at marketing and he knows that. He doesn't have the personality to mingle and charm the way I do. He's not resourceful; he can never get to the right people. That's why the business was plodding along at a five percent profit margin before I came along."

"Yes, and he's raking in fifteen percent and you're only getting one-tenth of that! If you're such a savvy businessman, tell him you want at least another twenty percent. For God's sakes, Ben, we've been in the same damn rut for years! If you're the brains behind the organization, use them for a change. Demand that he give you more!"

For once he listened to her incessant badgering; he'd always turned it off before, and that was why he never knew what her beef really was. He'd simply given her a stack of credit cards, had his accountant pay the bills, and ignored her groaning about money. "Maybe she's right," he mumbled to himself, a habit since childhood. Dyslexic as a child, he read everything out loud. He then began verbalizing his thoughts, most of the time without even realizing it. Yes, something was telling him to stop and evaluate what she'd said. After all, it had been four years...

∽

"I'm sorry, Ben, I just can't." Roy shook his head, the stiffly sprayed, dyed pompadour gleaming in the sunlight. "I started the company with family money, and it's got to remain so. You know you'll get everything when I...you know."

"Come on, Roy," Ben urged. "You're still on the good side of sixty-five. And even though we both work hard, you should know by now that you wouldn't have any of these clients if it wasn't for my expert negotiating and diplomacy."

"You know how much I appreciate it, Ben, but I must say no. I'm sorry." Roy rose from his leather chair and headed out the glass sliding doors to stand on the balcony. He leaned over the railing at the sprawling city below him, a ritual he carried out every noontime.

"If you say so, Roy." Ben turned on a heel and walked out of the office slowly, his mind busily calculating Plan B.

"Well, did you ask him?" Ben's wife implored, following him on his heels down the hall and into the bedroom.

He slid out of his jacket and turned to face her, looking into the eyes that revealed undeniable frustration. "Don't worry, honey." He winked at her, loosening his tie and flicking it off. "You'll get everything you want. Just give me some time."

"Time! You've been at it four years and you never—"

"I said," he cut her off, cracking his tie like a whip inches from her face, "give me time. And don't bug me about this ever again, you hear?" Stalking away, he yanked the bathroom door open, locked himself inside and ran a hot shower.

Ben decided to give his senior partner one more chance to grant him more stock before taking action. The answer was the same it had been for the last four years: "I'm sorry, Ben, but..."

Your time's up, Ben thought. If you're sorry now, just wait and see just how sorry you'll be later.

Ridgefield, Ltd., their biggest client, graciously flew the two partners and their wives to the Christmas bash every year, an elegant evening of dining and entertainment in Dallas's posh Hyatt Regency. As Ridgefield's president made the traditional champagne toast, two hundred tuxedoed executives drank to another prosperous and profitable new year.

Ben watched out of the corner of his eye as his partner sipped at the bubbly liquid. Another sip, then another. Ben's eyes widened on cue when Roy began to gasp and sputter. Ben dashed over to catch the older man as he collapsed, unconscious.

Roy's wife shrieked. "Oh, Roy, no! Somebody help my husband. I think he's having a heart attack!"

The paramedics arrived and whisked Roy off to Parkland Hospital.

"It's all right, Mrs. White," Ben soothed the portly blonde matron sobbing into a lace handkerchief. "He'll be just fine, I'm sure." he mumbled, more to himself than to the frantic woman.

Roy lived to see the New Year and Ben spent the holiday blankly staring at football games on TV and devising Plan B-1. "Yeah, that's it!" he thought out loud, stuffing his mouth with Doritos. "It's got to work!"

"What's got to work?" his wife, accustomed to his verbalized thinking, asked him.

"Oh, nothing." He waved a dismissive hand as his mind's wheels spun. "Just a new marketing concept."

∼

Ben didn't have much time to be imaginative. He rented a nondescript brown sedan for a few nights and followed Roy's every move from five o'clock onwards. He parked on a dark side street behind the office building, sat in the driver's seat, and waited. He'd chosen a very suitable time of year; at five p.m. it was pitch black. At six-thirty-five, the distinguished executive walked down the front steps as always, preferring to walk around the building rather than use the rear exit.

"A-ha, there he is, right on target," Ben mumbled. Without taking his eyes off his partner, Ben turned the key in the ignition and the engine hummed into life. Watching as Roy headed towards him, he shifted into a low gear and let up on the brake. He nosed down the street at about a mile an hour, headlights off. All Roy could possibly hear was the humming of a distant engine, blending in with the roar of traffic on the main road behind him.

Roy approached the building's garage, his car parked about fifty feet from where Ben had stalked him.

"Let's go, baby, let's go, let's go!" Ben urged as Roy crossed the street diagonally, heading for his car. "Now!" a demonic voice screamed, and he floored the accelerator. His body arched forward with the car's sudden lurch. Lights sped by, dazzling him. As he sped down the street, he realized he'd completely missed Roy, and without headlights or taillights, he could see nothing in the inky blackness behind him. He slammed on the brakes a foot short of the busy intersection.

Traffic zipped across the busy 4-lane street. "Damn!" He pounded the steering wheel. "I blew it!"

Roy took the next day off and never mentioned the incident. Ben returned the car with nothing more than a bit of rubber burned off the tires.

Ben planned to wait a safe length of time before instigating Plan B-2, so no one would be suspicious of Roy's accident-prone tendencies of late.

Ben phoned his wife to tell her he'd be tied up in meetings, but her voice mail picked up. After leaving her a message, he waited until 5:30, ate a sandwich at Subway, and returned to the office at seven. He entered the dark building, walked up to the second floor, flipped on the hallway light switch, and entered Roy's empty office. The phone began to ring as he entered but he knew the answering machine would pick up.

The caller left his name, number, and time of the call. Not wanting to turn the office light on, Ben flipped his pocket flashlight on and aimed a weak beam at Roy's cluttered desk. The cone of light scanned the array of pens, file folders, and stacks of Wall Street Journals. He raised the torch and aimed it at the glass sliding doors. The reflection beamed back at him like a beacon. He stepped forward, unlatched the lock and opened the slider. "A-ha." He licked his lips in glee. "How about some nice fresh air, Roy?"

Positioning the flashlight on its side so that it shone on the balcony railing, he crossed the office to retrieve the bag in which he'd brought the tools of his trade: screwdriver, pliers, wrench. On the way back to the balcony, he tripped and crashed head first into Roy's desk. The damn answering machine wire! He stumbled and fell squarely on the machine, hitting his head on the desk top, arms splayed protectively before him. The mechanism hummed inside the machine as he let out a string of curses. He groped in his bag for the simple tools that would put Roy White out of business—permanently.

After about two minutes, he walked out to the balcony and in the dim haze of the flashlight, loosened the screws holding the railing to the wall. "This is it, partner," he muttered, "the poison didn't bury you and the car didn't flatten you, but when you take that noontime lean on this balcony," his sinister cackle echoed through the empty office, "you'll see the clouds all right —except you'll see them looking down from the pearly gates."

His task completed, he shut the slider, locked it, and gathered his tools. Sporting the same wide grin that had won over many a client, he left the building.

"Come in here, please." Roy's voice, a bit more gruff than usual, betrayed a shakiness Ben had never detected in his partner's tone.

"Are you all right?" Ben rushed into Roy's office. "What's up? You look as if you've seen a ghost!" And he did. His face was paler than the pages of his desk calendar open on his desk. The man looked stricken.

"It's just occurred to me, Ben, that there has been some foul play around here. Someone wants to do me in." His eyes met Ben's, crossing as they focused.

Tensing his muscles to keep from trembling, Ben glanced out the window and fiddled with his tie. "Oh, come on, Roy, you've been reading too many of those murder mysteries. How melodramatic. 'Someone wants to do me in,'" he mimicked his partner's voice, exaggerating the quality of doom and foreboding. "Who would want to do a thing like that and why?"

After he spoke, he regretted he'd phrased it quite that way, knowing he'd left himself wide open for the answer he dreaded:

"Who and why?" He leveled a narrow-eyed stare at ben. "You are the who and money is the why."

He blanched. "Roy, how can you..." Damn. He cursed himself for not having rehearsed this. How to react? Insulted? Hurt? Go on the defensive? He ad-libbed it, simply by letting Roy continue.

"I became suspicious after the hit-and-run attempt, Ben, my boy. I hoped, as God is my witness, I hoped it wasn't you; the man I'd depended on and trusted all these years. I'd hoped that filthy rotten money didn't mean that much to you. But I had to make sure. After all, you'd been so patient and cooperative up to now, living with your ten per cent. But to make sure, I hired someone to investigate these bizarre happenings. And something was found." He paused. Ben held his breath. "I was able to catch the plate number of the sedan that almost ran me over, and I'm sure it can be traced to you, especially after I heard the expletives you uttered when you tripped over the cord there," he pointed to the abhorrent black cord running across the floor up to the blasted answering machine, "and the incriminating phrases you divulged when you did your dirty work on the balcony. You threw the switch that activates the message recorder and recorded your own voice. I retrieved two messages on the machine, one directly before and one directly after your break-in. One was at 7:05 and the other was at 7:15, which gave you exactly ten minutes to set your trap and abscond. You should try to confine your thoughts to your mind, Ben, and make sure it's in gear before engaging your tongue, because I've really got you this time."

Struck numb, Ben sank into the nearest chair, unable to meet his partner's eyes.

"But, I'm not going to press charges, Ben. I'd be spiting myself if I did that. You've been right all along, my friend. I do need you for this business. I know you've been doing a fantastic job. As a matter of fact, I was going to hand you another twenty-five per cent of the company at Christmas to finally grant you your wish. And if you think I'm bluffing, ask my wife. She entered the motion in the corporate book. But, no, you wanted me dead so you could get it all, not just a measly twenty-five per cent. You couldn't wait a few more years till I went naturally to get it all. It had to be now."

Cold moisture seeped through Ben's suit jacket. He'd never sweated like this before. He shivered. Roy's eyes pinned him.

"Yes, Ben, I'm going to keep you on as a partner. In fact, I'm still going to give you that twenty-five per cent at Christmas. Because I know you're a hard worker and I'd be nowhere without you. I'd also be nowhere if your plans hadn't fallen through, but that's beside the point. Now, I wrote a concise note which is in the hands of my attorney. It states that you, Benjamin Blanchard, have tried on three separate occasions to kill me. The incriminating tape is with the note. It states further that if I happen to meet my death in any way resembling foul play or suspicion, that the police be contacted immediately, and you be charged with my murder. Do you have anything more to say, Ben?"

Ben shook his head, the numbness creeping to the roots of his hair. He kicked at the wire, that hateful wire, as if it were a cockroach.

"Well?" Roy's lips spread in a half-smile, half-smirk. "What have you got to say for yourself?"

Ben screwed up his mouth and muttered between tightly clenched teeth, "You got me, partner. I'm turning a new leaf as of this minute and will repent. May you—and God—forgive me."

∾

At two o'clock the next morning, a shadowy figure emerged from under Roy White's Mercedes. Wiping the grease from his hands, he turned to the portly platinum blonde matron standing beside him draped in a quilted lounging gown.

"Half now, half when the job's finished," he whispered, although they were the only two people on the empty street.

She handed him a bulging envelope. "See me tomorrow for the other half, Lou," she murmured, turned, and entered her house.

∾

The policeman arrived at Ben Blanchard's doorstep just after his second cup of coffee the next morning.

Ben was stunned to see the two imposing uniforms blocking the light in his doorway. "Houston Police."

"What is all this about, officers?" Ben's heart hammered.

"Mr. Benjamin Blanchard?" the larger of the two asked, flashing his badge.

"Yes..."

"Roy White was killed last night when his brakes failed on the 610 Loop. You're under arrest for his murder. Bill, read him his rights."

Dear reader,

We hope you enjoyed reading *Murder By Moonlight*. Please take a moment to leave a review, even if it's a short one. Your opinion is important to us.

Discover more books by Diana Rubino at
https://www.nextchapter.pub/authors/diana-rubino

Want to know when one of our books is free or discounted for Kindle? Join the newsletter at
http://eepurl.com/bqqB3H

Best regards,
Diana Rubino and the Next Chapter Team

Manufactured by Amazon.ca
Bolton, ON